CHRISTMAS IN THE TRENCHES

To my sons, Will and Peter. And to all young men and women who challenge the past and change the future.

—*J. M.*

To Victoria, Triatan, and Lille Bedstefar

—*H. S.*

Published by
PEACHTREE PUBLISHERS
1700 Chattahoochee Avenue
Atlanta, Georgia 30318-2112

www.peachtree-online.com

Text © 2006 by John McCutcheon

Illustrations © 2006 by Henri Sørensen

Book design by Loraine M. Joyner

Illustrations created in oil on canvas. Title, bylines, initial capitals, and headings typeset in Esselte Letraset Ltd.'s Willow; main text typeset in Goudy Infant from dtpTypes Limited.

Printed and manufactured in Singapore
10 9 8 7 6 5 4 3 2 1
First Edition

ISBN 1-56145-374-9

Library of Congress Cataloging-in-Publication Data

McCutcheon, John.
  Christmas in the trenches / written by John McCutcheon ; illustrations by Henri Sørensen.– 1st ed.
    p. cm.
  Summary: A World War I veteran tells his grandson of his experiences in 1914, when British and German soldiers declared a truce from fighting to celebrate Christmas together.
  ISBN 1-56145-374-9
  1. Christmas Truce, 1914–Juvenile fiction. [1. Christmas Truce, 1914–Fiction. 2. World War, 1914-1918–Fiction. 3. Christmas–Fiction. 4. Grandfathers–Fiction.] I. Sorensen, Henri, ill. II. Title.
  PZ7.M139914Chr 2006
  [Fic]–dc22
                                    2006002710

CHRISTMAS IN THE TRENCHES

STORY BY
JOHN McCUTCHEON

ILLUSTRATIONS BY
HENRI SØRENSEN

Ω

PEACHTREE
ATLANTA

The presents had been opened and dinner was over. After a long walk through the snow-covered fields, young Thomas Tolliver curled up next to his grandfather and announced, "Grandpa, this was my very favorite Christmas. Do you have a favorite Christmas?"

"Yes, Thomas, I do," said Grandpa Francis. "I was far away from our home here in Liverpool. It was a Christmas many years ago during the first winter of the Great War."

"You were in the war, Grandpa?" chirped little Nora, climbing onto his lap. "What was it like? Were you a hero?"

Grandpa smiled.

"Let's see," he said. "Why don't I start at the beginning?"

The two children snuggled closer.

"It was 1914. My mates and I had been on the battlefield for many weeks…

We were all so young…just boys…
lonely and frightened, trying to be brave.
We had spent a long, cold month
in the muddy trenches that
were now our home.
We all knew that there
would be no break
in the fighting. We
knew we would be
spending Christmas
in the trenches.

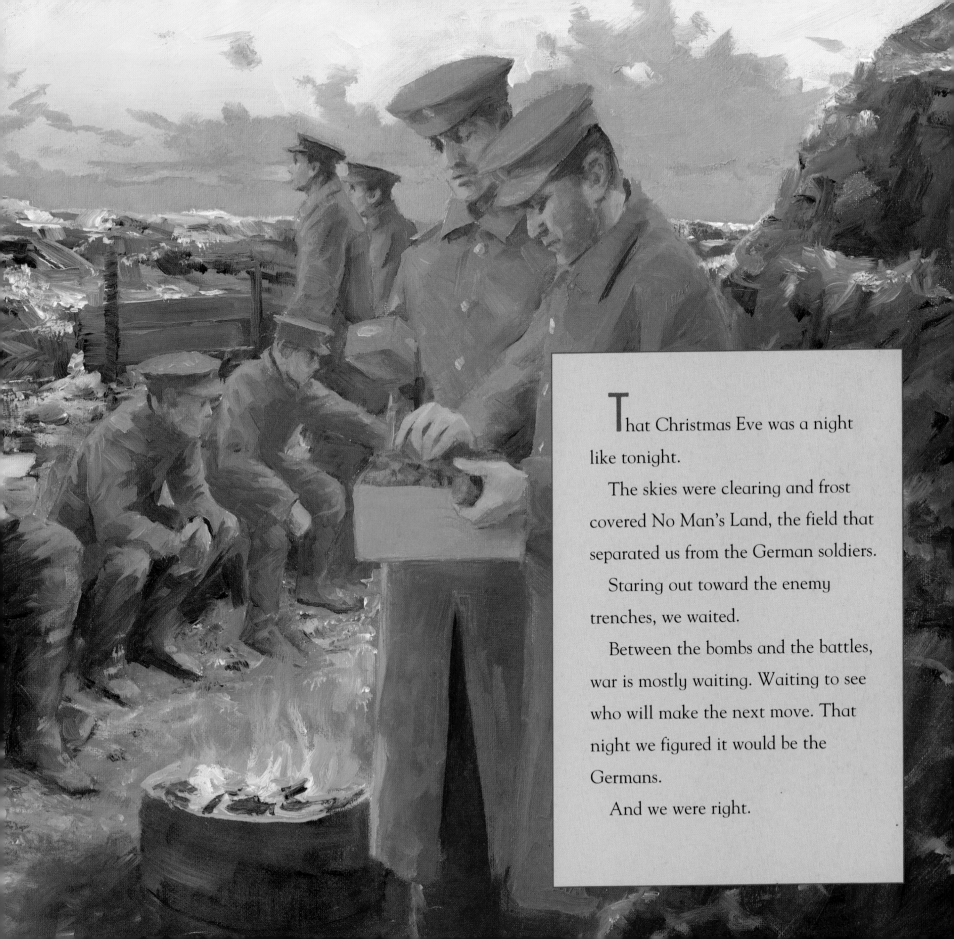

That Christmas Eve was a night like tonight.

The skies were clearing and frost covered No Man's Land, the field that separated us from the German soldiers.

Staring out toward the enemy trenches, we waited.

Between the bombs and the battles, war is mostly waiting. Waiting to see who will make the next move. That night we figured it would be the Germans.

And we were right.

Suddenly a sentry signaled for silence. We all hushed.
A ghostly sound cut through the cold night air.

Singing! It was coming from the enemy's side of No Man's Land!

One of the lads who knew German said, "It's a Christmas carol. He's singing right well, you know…" Soon, it seemed, every German voice joined in.

When they were finished, what could we do? We sang right back at them! "God Rest Ye Merry, Gentlemen."

All of us knew that one.

Then they sang something familiar.
We couldn't understand the words…
Stille Nacht…but we knew the melody.
It was "Silent Night."
And suddenly in two tongues one song
filled the night sky. I never imagined
singing could seem so…holy.

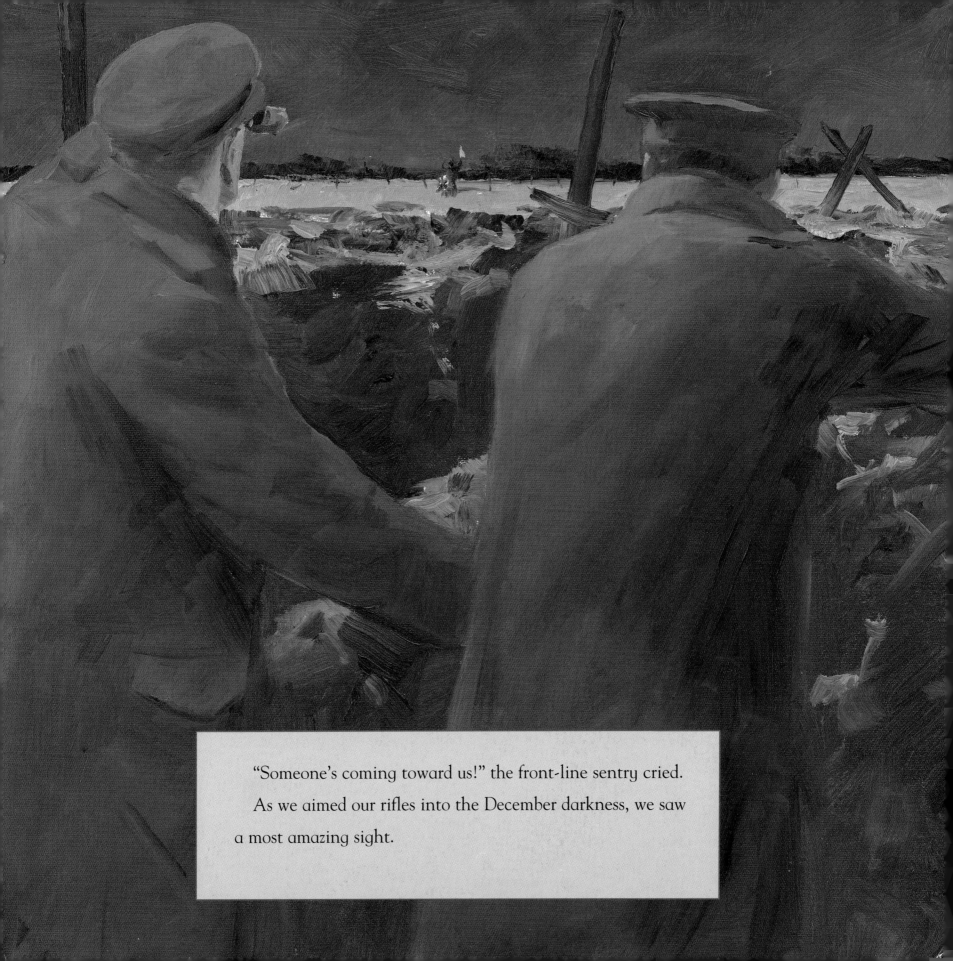

"Someone's coming toward us!" the front-line sentry cried.

As we aimed our rifles into the December darkness, we saw
a most amazing sight.

A single figure was coming across No Man's Land. In one hand he held a white truce flag, in the other a Christmas tree shining with candles.

It was so surprising and so brave I couldn't help myself. I leapt from the trench and walked toward him.

I was the first one. But soon everyone else from both sides was out there too.

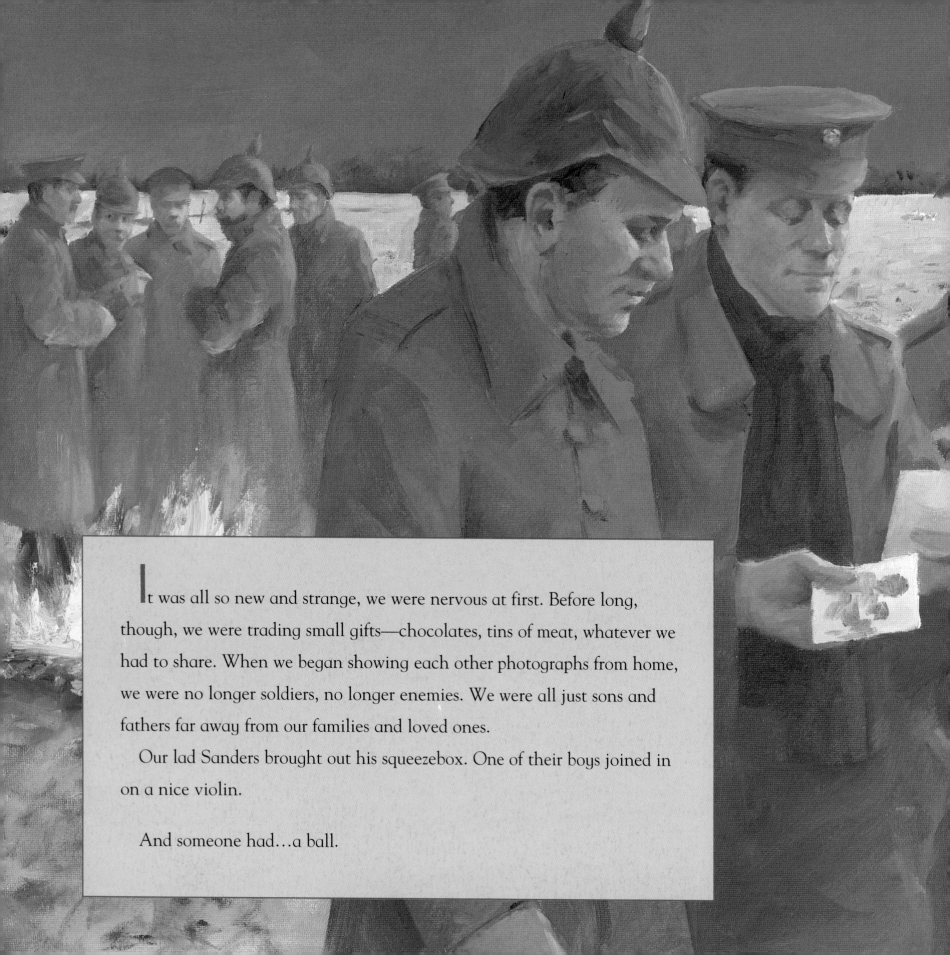

It was all so new and strange, we were nervous at first. Before long, though, we were trading small gifts—chocolates, tins of meat, whatever we had to share. When we began showing each other photographs from home, we were no longer soldiers, no longer enemies. We were all just sons and fathers far away from our families and loved ones.

Our lad Sanders brought out his squeezebox. One of their boys joined in on a nice violin.

And someone had…a ball.

It was quite the Christmas party we had! But all too soon the dawn reminded us it was time to get back to our own sides.

Back to the trenches.

Back to the waiting.

Wondering what had just happened to us and wondering what the next move should be.

That is my favorite memory—that Christmas in the trenches. I'm a different man today because of the boy I was that night."

Grandpa hugged the children tighter.

"Was I a hero? Ah…for just one night, yes. We were all heroes."

AUTHOR'S NOTE

I FIRST HEARD ABOUT the 1914 Christmas truce from a backstage janitor at a Birmingham, Alabama concert hall in 1984. I was so taken with this woman's story, I wrote the entire song "Christmas in the Trenches" during the intermission of my concert that night.

Though the story is true—there really was a Christmas truce, in fact, there were many of them in 1914 and again in 1915—I made no attempt to be historically accurate. I invented the main character in the song, named him Francis Tolliver, decided that he should be from Liverpool, England, and placed him in the trenches that freezing December night in 1914. I simply tried to tell his story so anyone listening would feel that they were there with him. The song almost wrote itself.

I first thought I would only sing the song and tell the story during the Christmas season. I soon learned it deserves—no, needs—to be told 365 days a year.

I knew all along that this was more than a story about peace breaking out in the middle of war. But why, I wondered, does it touch people so deeply? Was it because it also conveys a lesson about being human in a most inhumane situation? Because it demonstrates that bravery is about more than facing danger? Because it illustrates the power of our similarities rather than the division of our differences?

Wars don't start on battlefields. They begin in people's hearts. And that is where wars can be ended.

I believe we need to begin learning how to wage peace at a very early age. Every child is the beginning of a whole new world. Children learn about wars and generals in their schools almost from the first day. However, many programs teaching the skills of nonviolence, conflict resolution, and peacemaking are available for schools, youth groups, and families. I will keep an ever-updated list of some of them at this website:

http://folkmusic.com/f_peace.htm

What can one kid, one family, one classroom, one group of people do? One starry night nearly a hundred years ago one lonely soldier thought of home, of Christmas, and sang a carol from his trench in a muddy field. His buddies heard and joined in. Across that muddy field their enemies added their voices to the chorus. And all these years later we still have a chance to listen…and to join in.

Shalom, Salaam, Frieden, Peace!

John McCutcheon

HISTORICAL NOTE

Although CHRISTMAS IN THE TRENCHES is a fictional account, the Christmas Truce of 1914 really happened. It was a series of events occurring along the front line that stretched over 400 miles, through eastern France, from the Belgian coast in the north to the Swiss border in the south.

Four months earlier at the start of World War I (or the Great War, as it came to be known), millions of men from all over Europe had responded enthusiastically to the calls of their leaders to enlist. Most people believed it would be a short war, sure to be over by Christmas. But as winter began, thousands of soldiers had been killed or wounded and the ugly reality of the battlefield had set in.

By December 1914, the Allied forces (Belgium, France, and Britain) were locked in a stalemate with the Germans, each side hoping to wait the other out. The troops were shielded by hastily dug trenches. These narrow ditches, although deeper than the height of a standing soldier, provided little protection from the bitter cold of that winter.

Between the two armies was a barren stretch of ground called No Man's Land, generally wider than the length of two football fields. In some places, only 30 yards separated the entrenched troops. In these spots, they were so near that soldiers on one side could hear their enemies on the other side talking.

From such close quarters, many of the troops must have wondered what the men across the way were really like. Were they content to be stuck in these cold, muddy trenches fighting in the name of the Kaiser or the Queen, or wouldn't they prefer to be at home? As Christmas Eve approached, many soldiers must have been thinking about home and peace. Some had received packages from their families filled with holiday offerings. Even the royal families of Britain and Germany had shipped gifts to their troops. And Germany had sent Christmas trees to their men on the front lines.

All along the trenches, remarkable things began to happen. In the midst of a terrible war, men willed the fighting to stop, even if only for a few hours. As many as 100,000 may have participated in the unofficial truces that Christmas.

Some recorded eyewitness accounts in diaries and letters.

Albert Moren, a seventeen-year-old British private, wrote:
> It was a beautiful moonlit night, frost on the ground, white almost everywhere; and...there was a lot of commotion in the German trenches and then there were those lights— I don't know what they were. And then they sang "Silent Night"—*Stille Nacht.*

Corporal John Ferguson, a Scotsman, wrote:
> ...What a sight—little groups of Germans and British extending almost the length of our front!... Where they couldn't talk the language they were making themselves understood by signs, and everyone seemed to be getting on nicely. Here we were laughing and chatting to men whom only a few hours ago we were trying to kill!

Kurt Zehmisch, a German soldier, wrote in his diary:
> The English brought a soccer ball from the trenches, and pretty soon a lively game ensued. How marvelously wonderful, yet how strange it was. The English officers felt the same way about it. Thus Christmas, the celebration of Love, managed to bring mortal enemies together as friends for a time.

The two definitive references about the Christmas Truce are SILENT NIGHT by Stanley Weintraub (Free Press, 2001; Penguin, 2002, expanded paperback edition) and CHRISTMAS TRUCE by Malcolm Brown and Shirley Seaton (Pan Macmillan Ltd, 1994, expanded paperback edition) both of which were used in developing this note.

For more information about the truce and World War I, including additional references, visit our website at *www.christmasinthetrenches.info*.

CHRISTMAS IN THE TRENCHES

BY JOHN McCUTCHEON

My name is Francis Tolliver, I come from Liverpool.
Two years ago the war was waiting for me after school.
To Belgium and to Flanders, to Germany to here,
I fought for King and country I love dear.

'Twas Christmas in the trenches where the frost so bitter hung.
The frozen fields of France were still, no Christmas song was sung.
Our families back in England were toasting us that day,
Their brave and glorious lads so far away.

I was lying with my messmate on the cold and rocky ground,
When across the lines of battle came a most peculiar sound.
Says I, "Now listen up, me boys!" Each soldier strained to hear,
As one young German voice sang out so clear.

"He's singing bloody well, you know!" my partner says to me.
Soon, one by one, each German voice joined in harmony.
The cannons rested silent, the gas clouds rolled no more,
As Christmas brought us respite from the war.

As soon as they were finished and a reverent pause was spent,
"God Rest Ye Merry, Gentlemen" struck up some lads from Kent.
The next they sang was "Stille Nacht." "Tis 'Silent Night'," says I,
And in two tongues one song filled up that sky.

"There's someone coming toward us!" the front line sentry cried.
All sights were fixed on one lone figure trudging from their side.
His truce flag, like a Christmas star, shown on that plain so bright
As he bravely strode unarmed into the night.

Soon one by one on either side walked into No Man's Land,
With neither gun nor bayonet we met there hand to hand.
We shared some secret brandy and we wished each other well,
And in a flare-lit soccer game we gave 'em hell.

We traded chocolates, cigarettes, and photographs from home,
These sons and fathers far away from families of their own.
Young Sanders played his squeezebox and they had a violin,
This curious and unlikely band of men.

Soon daylight stole upon us and France was France once more.
With sad farewells we each prepared to settle back to war.
But the question haunted every heart that lived that wondrous night,
"Whose family have I fixed within my sights?"

'Twas Christmas in the trenches where the frost so bitter hung.
The frozen fields of France were warmed as songs of peace were sung.
For the walls they'd kept between us to exact the work of war
Had been crumbled and were gone forevermore.

My name is Francis Tolliver, in Liverpool I dwell.
Each Christmas come since World War I, I've learned its lessons well.
That the ones who call the shots won't be among the dead and lame,
And on each end of the rifle we're the same.